Urgency
and Patience

Jean-Philippe Toussaint

Urgency and Patience

translated from the French
by Edward Gauvin

DALKEY ARCHIVE PRESS
Champaign / London / Dublin

Originally published in French as
L'urgence et la patience
Copyright © 2012 Jean-Philippe Toussaint
Translation © 2014 Edward Gauvin
First edition, 2015
All rights reserved

LIBRARY OF CONGRESS CATALOGING-IN-PUBLICATION DATA

Toussaint, Jean-Philippe.
 [Essays. Selections. English]
 Urgency and patience / Jean-Philippe Toussaint ;
translated by Edward Gauvin. -- First edition.
     pages cm
 "Originally published in French as L'urgence et la
patience"--Title page verso.
 ISBN 978-1-62897-079-1 (pbk. : alk. paper)
 I. Gauvin, Edward, translator. II. Title.

PQ2680.O86A2 2015
844'.914--dc23

                                    2014031428

Partially funded by a grant by the Illinois Arts Council

This translation was funded with the support of Ministère
de la Fédération Wallonie-Bruxelles

www.dalkeyarchive.com
Cover: design & composition by Mikhail Iliatov
Printed on permanent / durable & acid-free paper

Urgency
and Patience

To my parents, who taught me to read and write.

Author's Note

Some of the pieces here are new to this collection; others first appeared in periodicals (the Japanese literary reviews *Littéraire* and *Subaru*, the French review *Constructif*, the Swiss German paper *Neue Zürcher Zeitung*, the Belgian online literary review *Bon à tirer*). Others first appeared in books as interviews ("I, Rodion Romanovich Raskolnikov" in Flammarion's classroom standard edition of *Crime and Punishment*), accompaniments ("The Ravanastron" in *Objects*, a catalogue for the Beckett exhibit at the Centre Pompidou), off-prints ("Reading Proust" in a volume of a new Japanese translation of *In Search of Lost Time*), postfaces ("The Day I Met Jérôme Lindon" in the Minuit pocket edition of *The Bathroom*), and prefaces ("In Bus 63" in the Norwegian Library of World Literature edition of Beckett's trilogy). The essay "My Offices" consists of excerpts from the book *Mes bureaux, luoghi dove scrivo*, published by Editions Amos in Italy in 2005. All texts have been re-read and sometimes amended for the current edition.

The author would like to thank the Belgian Service for the Promotion of Letters, run by Jean-Luc Outers from 1990 to 2011, for its constant support.

The Day
I Began to Write

I've forgotten the precise hour of the exact day I decided to start writing, but that hour exists, and that day exists; that decision, the decision to start writing, is one I made abruptly, on a Paris bus, between place de la République and place de la Bastille.

I no longer have the slightest idea what I'd been doing earlier that day, for my memory of that very real day in September or October of 1979 has merged with my memory of the first paragraph of the book I wrote, which tells of how a man walking down a sunny street recalls the day he discovered the game of chess, a book that began—how well I remember, for it was the first sentence I ever wrote—with the words: "It was a bit of an accident that I discovered the game of chess." What I know with greater certainty—the memory grows clearer now—is that, when I got home that day, that Monday—I don't know if it was really a Monday, but I like to think so, I've always had a soft spot for Mondays—I wrote the first sentence of my first book in my room on the rue des Tournelles, with my back to the door, facing the wall. I wrote the first draft of that book in a month, on an old typewriter, and since I didn't yet know how to type, I picked my way clumsily along with two fingers (writing and learning to type at the same time).

The decision I made that day was rather unexpected for me. I was twenty (or twenty-one, who cares? I've always been a year off all my life), and I'd never before thought that I would someday write. I had no particular taste for reading; I read almost nothing (a Balzac here, a Zola there, that sort of thing). I read newspapers, a few humanities texts for my studies in history and political science. I wasn't interested in much of life: soccer, a little, and movies. As much pleasure as I'd taken in painting and drawing as a teen, I hadn't done much writing: no stories, no letters, next to nothing, not even a dozen of those awful poems all of us've written. The one thing in the world that interested me most of all back then was surely movies; I would very much have liked to make a film, if it hadn't been so hard to get it off the ground; yes, I could quite easily have seen myself as a director (I never saw myself as a politician, for instance). So I buckled down and wrote a little screenplay for a black-and-white silent short about a world chess championship whose victor would be whoever won ten thousand games: a championship that lasted a whole lifetime, consumed a whole lifetime, was no less than life itself, and ended with the death of all its protagonists (death interested me a great deal back then; it was one of my favorite subjects).

At the same time, in the same era, two books proved pivotal for me. The first was by François Truffaut, *The Films in My Life*, in which he advised all young people who dreamed of making movies, but lacked the means, to write a book, to turn their screenplay into a book, explaining that, just as movies required big budgets and entailed weighty responsibilities, so literature was a light, trifling activity, a joyous lark (I'm altering his words slightly), inexpensive (a ream of paper and a typewriter), which could be pursued in total freedom, at home or in the great outdoors, in a suit and tie or boxer shorts (which is how I wrote the end of *The Bathroom*: brow soaked with sweat, chest dripping, thighs damp, in the stifling shade of my house in Médéa, Algeria, where the temperature was pushing 104°F). The second pivotal read from that time was Dostoevsky's *Crime and Punishment*. That summer, on my sister's sound advice, I read *Crime and Punishment* for the first time. And, one month after that book, having known the frisson of identifying with the ambiguous character of Raskolnikov, I began to write. I'm not sure a direct connection need be sought, some perfect cause-and-effect relationship, or even—who knows?—a theorem (Whosoever reads *Crime and Punishment* shall start writing a month later), but that's how it was for me: one month after reading *Crime and Punishment*, I began to write—and I am writing still.

My Offices

I remember a character from Beckett—Molloy, or Malone—who planned to draw up an inventory of all his belongings and was always putting off the task. In my case, the task was instead to draw up an inventory of all the rooms where I've written in my life, the offices deliciously titillating my mind just then: from the bedroom on the rue des Tournelles in Paris, where I wrote my first book, *Échecs*, to the apartment in the administrative complex in Ain d'Heb, Médéa, where I wrote *The Bathroom*, by way of my offices in Corsica, in the "château" where I wrote *Monsieur*, but also in Erbalunga, in that little room in Prunete, that short-lived office in Cervione and the one in Corte, the office in Barcaggio, the office on the rue Saint-Sébastien in Paris, where I wrote the London part of *Camera*, the dark smoky office in Madrid where I drew the shutters to write *Reticence*, the handsome well-ventilated office in Berlin where I wrote the screenplay for *The Skating Rink*, not to mention various other fleeting or temporary offices in Amsterdam and Berlin, my elegant office in the Villa Kujoyama in Kyoto, my offices in Brussels and my offices in Ostend, the Résidence Vendôme and the Résidence Grenoble, in the big apartment across from the casino where I wrote the beginnings of *Making Love* and *Running Away*, and on the seventh floor of the Résidence Les Algues, where I wrote the first part of *The Truth about Marie*.

I didn't know then, but it was during my first major trip abroad that I really started writing. I've never mentioned Algeria in my books, or in any of my other writings afterwards, but it was during that sojourn in Algeria, from 1983 to 1984, that I finally found the necessary detachment, the right distance — several thousand miles lay between me and France — to conjure up Paris. This idea of distance seemed crucial to me. For distance requires a greater effort on the part of memory to mentally recreate the places we describe: having them right before our eyes — within eye's reach, so to speak — leads to a laziness in description, a lack of effort on the part of imagination, while being required to recreate a city and its lights from nothing — mere dream or remembrance — brings life and the power of conviction to the scenes we describe.

I never kept any of the rough drafts of *The Bathroom*; I burned them all before leaving Algeria, hundreds of sheets burned one evening at dusk in the public trash cans of the Aïn d'Heb complex a few days before I left. I remember my state of mind as I watched those drafts vanish in the flames, eyes shining though I wasn't sad, merely melancholy, like that September evening at Cinecittà when I looked out for a long time at the pale blue skies over Rome on the last day of shooting *The Skating Rink*, thinking simply that something quite beautiful was coming to an end.

As far back as I can remember, I've always felt a fascination for my grandfather's offices. He had one in Ostend, in the apartment my grandparents rented on the dike, a stone's throw from the old clock that has since been replaced. It wasn't really an office — rather, a simple work desk on which lay a few papers, scissors, glasses, a magnifying glass. But I remember best of all my grandfather's office in Sars-Dames-Avelines: a mysterious room, often locked, which we children never entered, a room which, in truth, I have no actual memory of, neither sight nor smell, but which I cling to like an absolute memory, mythic and formative. As if that room, my grandfather's office in Sars-Dames-Avelines, were the one I wished to reconstruct, to recreate unconsciously in the various houses where I've lived since then: that room with its smell of old paper and books, its calm and its silence, that fascinating room where one could think and write, that room which was a defense against the world outside, a shelter, a refuge, a bathroom.

Urgency and Patience

When I'm writing a book, I want to be airborne, breezy of mind and blithe of hand ... My ass. Actually, I'm very organised. I train myself, prepare myself, prime myself. There's something monastic in my mindset, something Spartan, something of the lonely sailor. Everything matters: physical fitness, diet, reading. When I'm writing, I go to bed early and don't drink. During the day, I walk, I bike, I swim—swimming has never failed to complement study, quite the opposite in fact. Until *Reticence*, whenever I embarked on a book, I would work all day, every day, without coming up for air, without taking a break, up to a year at a time. I thought of writing as heavy machinery set up for the long haul; something steady, heavy, hindersome; something that refused to budge, that stumbled, that progressed effortfully, inch by inch—a plow.

The painful experience of writing *Reticence*, a book I was not managing to write, a book I almost gave up on several times—I was mired, I couldn't muddle through, but I gritted my teeth, kept digging, held on, calling upon the figure of Kafka and the most self-flagellating ideals of writing—this painful experience led to my decision never to write this way again. I no longer wanted to suffer like this, I had to change my method. From then on, I have only worked when the impetus has taken me, in writing sessions of limited duration, for a fortnight to three months at most, punctuated by long periods when I did something else—not writing, living—which has its uses, too.

> I've always had remarkable success with this sort of mental labour, it's true, letting the book come to gradually settle in and inhabit me by simply following the thread of my thoughts, doing nothing that might interrupt the flow, and so unchaining a multitude of impressions and reveries, a host of structures and ideas, often incomplete, scattered, unformed, some still gestating, some already fully developed, a wealth of intuitions and insights, of pains and emotions, which I then had only to put into their definitive form ... And ... I reflected that, if your goal is to write, not writing is surely at least as important as writing.*

Until *Reticence*, it would take me about a year to write a book, but now the same number of actual working hours is spread out over three instead. I work not at home, in Brussels, but in Corsica, or Ostend. In Ostend, I rent an apartment, a neutral space; I like the hermit crab aspect of a guest who moves into a shell that doesn't belong to him. The places where I work are always temporary, put to other uses in my absence. Sometimes other people live

---

* *Television*, trans. Jordan Stump, (Dalkey Archive, 2004)

in the Ostend apartment, and the large room where I write in Corsica serves another purpose when I'm not there. I show up, claim these places for myself, set up shop: computer, printer, research. When I go, I take everything with me, and leave no traces of my passage.

I like the idea that a book can be defined as a "dream in stone" (the words are Baudelaire's). "Dream" because of the freedom it demands—daring, risk, fantasy, the unknown; "stone" because of the consistency—firm, solid, mineral—obtained through sheer, unrelenting work on language, words, and grammar. When you've got your nose too deep in a manuscript, your eyes in the gears and grease of sentences, sometimes you lose sight of the line of a book. Now, I like picturing a book as a line. I like the abstraction of it, where literature meets music, and the line of a book rises, falls, billows at the pure whim of rhythm. Sometimes a contradiction arises between my desire to write lasting sentences, akin to aphorisms, and the need for such sentences not to interrupt reading, not even to slow it down. These sentences must be swept up in the course of the novel without disturbing its flow, must burrow into the text, almost camouflaged, so that they sparkle without drawing too much attention. When, at the end of a climactic scene, the book soars and reaches a summit, how to continue the narration, how to come back down, without losing one's grip on the reader? Must the line of a book always be a constant crescendo from first to last? No, one can install accelerandos inside individual parts, play with breaks in rhythm, make the last line of a paragraph resound. All these things can be calculated, meted out, and measured. These are technical questions, matters of craft. A book must seem self-evident to a reader, and not something premeditated or constructed. But this self-evidence is something the writer himself must construct.

There are always, I believe, two seemingly irreconcilable notions at play in writing: urgency and patience.

Urgency, which calls on impulse, ardor, speed — and patience, which requires slowness, steadfastness, and effort. And yet both are indispensable to writing a book: in varying proportions, distinct doses, every writer working out an individual alchemy, one or the other of these traits being dominant and the other recessive, like alleles that decide the color of one's eyes. And so, among writers, there are the urgent and the patient, those in whom urgency dominates (Rimbaud, Faulkner, Dostoyevsky), and those in whom patience prevails — Flaubert, of course, patience itself.

Usually, urgency presides over the writing of a book, and patience is but its indispensable complement, which allows for the later correction of the manuscript's early drafts. In Proust, it would seem that patience precedes urgency. Proust does not write the first draft of *In Search of Lost Time*; he simply lives, taking all the time he wants, as if re-reading it before ever writing it. Patience is his life and urgency his body of work. But every personal conception of the act of writing is a unique neurosis. Every night, Kafka would sit down at his desk and wait for the impetus that would bring him to write. He had this faith in literature; it was all he believed in, all he wanted ("I cannot nor do I want to be any other thing"), and every night he thought this inaccessible ideal—writing—would happen for him. Indeed, sometimes it did. He wrote "The Judgment" in one night, and *The Metamorphosis* would be written in the same state of grace. Beside these nights of fever and urgency, the practice of writing was, for Kafka, an arid daily quest. Nothing ever came, not ever. Day after day, he wrote in his *Diaries*: "Today I wrote nothing." I loved Kafka's *Diaries* so much; I devoured them passionately, lived on them, went back to them time and again, studied, annotated, meditated on them. Some sentences in the *Diaries* are terrible, cruel, lucid; all are moving: "Uncertainty, drought, silence, it will all pass away."

Patience

In writing a book, everything always begins and ends with patience. Beforehand, the book must be left to steep in itself: this is the ripening phase, when the first images occur, characters are sketched. You gather research, take notes, work out an early plan of the whole in your head. With this preparatory phase carried to its extremity, the danger lies in never starting the novel (Barthes' syndrome, in a way), like the narrator of *Television* who, due to exaggerated scruples and anxiety from the exigencies of perfectionism, settles for a constant state of readiness to write "without taking the easy way out and actually doing so". For, however essential it is to hold on to a text at length, letting go one day is also indispensable, after all. Afterwards, as soon as a page is finished, you print it out and read it over, amend, cross out, draw arrows all over, correct, add a few handwritten lines, check a word, rework a turn of phrase. Then you print the page out again and start all over, re-correct, re-check, then reprint and reread, and so on, to infinity, hunting down errors and flushing out dross, until the final paring in the proofs.

I like that moment at dawn when one cautiously opens the manuscript of a book in progress, in a house still asleep. There are several strategies for trying to see the work with a fresh eye, to surprise it, snare it, catch it unawares, as if coming across it for the first time, in order to judge it with an unbiased eye. A nap can do the trick; a good night's sleep is even better. I even suspect that part of reading a book over can happen during sleep. When you're awake, a book etches itself into the brain with the precision of a chess position, but when you sleep at night, the study of variants continues, as if in a computer left on to examine the immensity of the calculations in play in the process (such that sometimes a solution will occur to me on waking without any particular conscious effort). But no point doggedly deleting without end; only time truly cleanses and renews one's vision. According to Palma the Younger, Titian always turned his paintings to the wall for months at a time without looking at them. Then, when he took them up again, "he would examine them with strict attention, as if they had been his mortal enemies." Ah, dearest mortal enemies!

"How, in such conditions, can I write, to consider only the manual aspect of that bitter folly?" Beckett wonders. Of my first typewriters, few memories now remain: there was a little clockwork orange one on which I wrote my first book, *Échecs*. But my first real typewriter, my beauty, my one and only, the thought of which still brings tears to my eyes (crocodile, oh crocodile), was my big fat Olivetti ET121—so beautiful, so efficient, and so very sophisticated that the instructions assumed it was meant only for secretaries or professional typists and were exclusively addressed to female users. *The proper Miss Typist must remember, the proper Miss Typist never forgets* . . . and I complied, intimidated, delighted, blushing, trembling, over the next ten years giving the best of myself—with two fingers. With this darling machine—but what am I saying?—*on* this darling machine, I wrote *The Bathroom*, *Monsieur*, *Camera*, *Reticence*. Where is she now? Abandoned, I imagine, on the scrapheap. O cruel fate! I see her still, in her native splendour, that darling fat old Olivetti, sitting on my desk in Médéa when, in the early hours of that sunny afternoon in 1983, I removed it from its packaging and peeled back the copious kapok padding, the different strata of transparent plastic, and delicately delivered it from its silk vestments and dust-cover of embroidered lace (I exaggerate, but only slightly). I can see her now, sitting on the desk of my office in Médéa ready to give herself to me, black and massive, elegant, silent and unmoving, with — to prop the paper up — a transparent windshield streamlined like a 1950s Italian convertible.

These days, I only ever use my computer. Before setting out, I gather my things into a soft-sided briefcase, for a while black but now a dark velvety blue, like a mobile office, a portable arsenal, which I take with me to Ostend or Corsica, with my MacBook Pro, which succeeds two white iBooks and two grayish, disappointing PowerBooks (one went completely autistic, refusing to print anymore, and the other expired in my arms with just enough time, in its dying breath, to surrender the contents of its hard drive). I slide the computer carefully into my bag, with its various assorted wires and power cords, then add a mouse, sometimes a keyboard, a folder with my research, a dictionary recently gone digital, and the manuscript in progress. The complete manuscripts of my last few books don't add up to more than fifty pages. I work on dense pages overcrowded with characters, in a Helvetica-based font with minimal line spacing, which yields very solid blocks of text: barely readable, disheartening to re-read. I like it that way, because it forces me never to be satisfied, to be instead ever more demanding. I must, always and forever, keep cutting, clarify, simplify, to make the depressing blocks of text before me fluid, make them fly. But I know that when the text has donned its handsomest finery, when it's set in Times New Roman and laid out immaculately on the page in nicely spaced lines, I'll send it to Irène Lindon decked out in a cover blue as night, and that poor shrivelled thing I've sweated over for months will blossom in the light like a flower opening to the sun. The idea is to train under ever tougher conditions, not easing up till the day comes, to practice penalty kicks with ski boots on (the day you take the ski boots off, it's immediately easier, you'll see).

Before starting a book, I almost never make preparatory notes. A novel must already be underway in my mind so my thoughts can cling to an episode of an existing book, a gestating scene starting to emerge slowly from my mind, like those whitish shapes with blurry, shifting silhouettes we see emerging on ultrasounds. It's more during the writing phase that I take notes. Sometimes, in Ostend, I stop on the dike and exhume a notebook from my pocket, extricating it from vexingly crumpled tissues flecked with grains of sand, to scribble a few words quickly while standing on the dike in the wind and drizzle, or even occasionally a shower; how beautiful it is to see the idea I've just jotted down go instantly runny with rain.

I owned a whole collection of notebooks, notepads, and scratchpads made by Rhodia or Schleicher & Schuell, with orange covers and detachable pages, as well as several little square Chinese notebooks with elegant hard covers in black and red. I always took a few of these with me when I went out, slipping them into my pocket before leaving my study, gradually filling them with bits or fragments of sentences, thoughts and aphorisms, observations and remarks (the latter being generally only the more accurate expression of the next-to-latter), which as a rule I never made use of in my actual work. No matter how brilliant, an idea really wasn't worth keeping if you couldn't even remember it without writing it down, it seemed to me.[*]

I wrote these words more than fifteen years ago (in Ostend, already not far from where I'm sitting now), and there is nothing to add to them, except perhaps a few new notebooks to mention, my little Muji notebooks, so well-proportioned—darling little notebooks, A6 or passport-sized, supple, with covers of kraft brown or charcoal gray—and perhaps a word about my pens, felt-tips in fact, Mitsubishi Uni-ball EYEs with tungsten carbide roller balls, fine or micro point, usually black but sometimes blue. I have an entire set fanned out on my desk (I thought it was literature I loved, but goodness me, it was really office supplies all along!).

[*] *Television*, trans. Jordan Stump, (Dalkey Archive, 2004)

When I was writing my first books, I did almost no research. I wrote *The Bathroom* empty-handed. I'd been lent a copy of Pascal's *Pensées* so I could translate a passage on diversion into English, and I had to borrow a first-year biology book from a co-worker for some rudimentary octopus anatomy. But now, with the widespread expansion of the Internet, we have access to a truly encyclopedic wealth of knowledge on any subject in real time. In *The Truth about Marie*, I took great pains to describe the piece of furniture the characters were moving out of Marie's apartment in the middle of the night: the commode. But then I realised I didn't really care about planting an image of this piece of furniture in the reader's mind. It was the word itself, *le bahut*, that interested me, its scruffiness, its charming sonorities: as a *literary detail*, deliberate, visible, considered, and not the image it evoked, an *iconic detail*, to take up the distinction Daniel Arasse has proposed. In other words, it was important that readers hear the word, not that they see the object. My description of the commode, which allowed readers to picture it — but added nothing to hearing the word — was thus pointless, and I deleted it.

For *The Truth about Marie*, I had to do even more research than usual, since I was tackling several themes largely unfamiliar to me (heart attacks, horses, transporting living animals in cargo planes). For the horses, I bought an exhaustive *Horse Owner's Veterinary Handbook*. But I even did that one better: I went so far as to climb on a horse and go for a ride in the Corsican maquis in the summer of 2006. It was the first time in my life I'd ever been on a horse (how far we sometimes go for research!). For the heart attack, I skipped having one myself (self-sacrifice has its limits), preferring to call up a doctor friend instead, and invite him to a Brussels brasserie for lunch. A bit embarrassed at the table, not daring to reveal the scene I was imagining (in general, I don't much like talking about the books I'm in the middle of writing), I asked him in a low voice, not directly but in a roundabout way, coughing slightly and rubbing my fingers, as if informing him of some peculiar desiderata, whom to contact in case of a slight snafu—for example, if a heart attack should arise during sex? And who shows up at the apartment in such cases (police? rescue workers? firemen?)? It was during this lunch that I heard, for the first time, that ever so risqué word: defibrillation. The experience repeated itself a few months later, this time with an Air France captain in a restaurant in Paris, and all luncheon long, I listened attentively while filling my little notebook with adorable doodles.

Urgency

Urgency is fleeting, fragile, intermittent.

Urgency is not, as I conceive it, inspiration. What distinguishes the two is that inspiration is received and urgency acquired. In the myth of inspiration—that great romantic myth—is a passivity I find displeasing, wherein the writer—the inspired poet—is the plaything of some grace outside himself, God or Nature, who comes and lays a finger on his innocent brow. No. Urgency is no gift, but a quest. It is arrived at only through effort, built only through work; one must go to meet it, venture into its realm. For urgency indeed has a realm, an abstract, metaphorical place in those inner regions reached only after a long journey. Urgency must be attained through immersion. You must take the plunge, fill your lungs with air and then descend, leave the everyday world behind and dive into the book underway, as if to the bottom of the ocean. You don't reach the bottom right away; there are steps, stages of decompression. In the early phases of the descent, you can still feel the visible world above, still see it even, still draw inspiration from it. That means you haven't gone deep enough. You have to keep going, persevere. At 450 feet, you can barely see anything anymore, you start to make out new shadows; memories of real people fade away while fictive creatures appear and surround us, a swarm of living micro-organisms of various shapes and sizes. We are in a shadowy world between reality and fiction. We keep going down and, past 650 feet, not a single ray of sunlight reaches us now. We have come at last to the realm of urgency, the world of abyss, more than 75 trillion acres of darkness and silence where crushing pressure reigns and endless blind presences proliferate, infinitesimal potential lives in motion. Here we are, the right depth: now we have the necessary distance, the ideal detachment with which to *reconstruct the world*, to retranscribe, the depths of writing itself, everything we have taken in on the surface. Here, at the very heart of urgency, everything comes easily, floats free and lets go; actual sight is of no more use to us, but the inner eye widens, and a fictive, fabulous world appears in our minds. Our senses are alert, our perceptions heightened, our sensitivity intensified; a tipping takes place, a gushing, and out it all comes, sentences are born, flow, fall over each other, and everything is right, everything works out, everything gathers and fits together in this intimate darkness that is the inside of our very minds. But the tiniest thing—a speck of dust, a snag—and the whole process breaks down, bringing us back up to the surface, for urgency is fragile, and can flee us at any moment.

Urgency is a state of writing that can only be arrived at after infinite patience. It is the reward for that patience, its miraculous denouement. All the efforts we made in the name of our book were, in reality, only straining toward this singular moment when urgency bursts forth, when it all tips over, when it comes by itself, when the string keeps endlessly unwinding from the ball. As in tennis, after hours of practice in which every movement has been analysed, broken down, and put back together *ad infinitum*, but remains stiff, rigid, and soulless, there comes a moment, in the heat of a match, when you start letting your strokes go and pull off some things that would've been unimaginable before you'd warmed up, and were only made possible by the rigour and persistence of the practice that preceded it. At moments like these, *in the heat of writing*, there's nothing we can't try, everything works; we graze the net, we hit it just inside the lines, we find everything instinctively, every bodily posture, the ideal bend to the knee, the way to wind up and swing— everything is right, every image, every word, every adjective is a volley intercepted and returned—everything finds its exact place in the book.

That's all there is to writing a book: this alternation between phases of gush and perseverance. After weeks of being blocked while I was writing *The Truth about Marie*, suddenly Zahir was fleeing down the runway at Narita. The scansion that set in then; the words that raced out, driving forward, dashing after the purebred; the jerky, staccato rhythm of the sentence calqued on the horse's gallop—these have something to do with breathlessness. We—the author, the reader, the pursuers, the sentence—are literally breathless. Beside these scenes written in urgency are moments when all forward progress stops, when the winds have fallen, and we are irreparably becalmed. That is when we must persevere, hang on, grit our teeth, keep *not getting there*, for urgency keeps moving forward, keeps working underground, building up energy. There's always something exponential about writing a book; the third month of work is enriched by the preceding ones; the more constant the effort has been, the more intense the deliverance will be. We can even further whet the necessity of urgency by restraining our desire, forcing it back like a rubber band in a deliberate strategy of retention, to lend its forward impetus all possible power, so that when the dikes burst, the book sweeps everything away upon its flood.

How I Built Certain of My Hotels

I could close my eyes and conjure them up one by one, the hotels in my books, recall them, materialize them, recreate them; once more I see the little entrance of that hotel in Venice from *The Bathroom*, the dark, disquieting stairwells of the hotel in Sasuelo from *Reticence*; once more I see the long hallway on the sixteenth floor from *Making Love*; once more I see the corridor cluttered with tarps and paint cans in the hotel under construction from *Running Away*. Once more I see the empty lobbies and labyrinthine corridors. I barely have to close my eyes—I can close my eyes while keeping them open, maybe that's what writing is—and right away I find myself in the great empty lobby of the Tokyo hotel with its lighted crystal chandeliers.

There are hotels in almost all my books. I don't build them with the usual construction materials: no load-bearing walls, no beams, no scaffolding, hardly any bricks and cement, no glass, wood, or aluminum. I make do with little, a few color adjectives for the rooms, the curtains, the bedspreads ("The walls around me were humid and dirty, covered with old orange wallpaper that matched the dark flowers on the bedspread and curtains."). I don't draw up plans for my hotels before building them, but I almost always see them, as if in a dream; the hotels in my books are chimeras of images, memories, fantasies, and words.

There are always a few characters here and there in the hotels I've built, ghosts more or less inspired by real people I've run into in my travels: the front desk lady from the hotel in Venice, invisible chambermaids, bellhops in black livery and gold buttons with little black caps on their heads, made-up doormen in official finery, frock coats and gray vests, who keep watch before the doors of imaginary hotels. Alongside these barely sketched figures are the more solid lines of a few on the brink of becoming characters in a novel: my friend the bartender at the hotel in Venice, the man who owned the hotel in Sasuelo, the woman who owned the hotel L'Ape Elbana in Portoferraio. One might recall similarities between some of my hotels, between the lobby of the hotel in Venice and that of the Hotel Hansen in Shanghai; one might note ley lines, points in common, Oriental coincidences, Mediterranean convergences—perhaps a style might emerge, the rooms take on recurrent motifs, a little flight of steps might be shared by several books. I could have begun a sentence in Madrid in the early '90s and ended it in Corsica fifteen years later:

A little flower-lined staircase led up to the hotel entrance with a double glass door. I walked up the steps at the entrance and crossed through an arbor under which white tableclothed tables had been set for breakfast.

The little flower-lined staircase would be the same, issued from an ageless imagination. But the first sentence is from *Reticence* (1991), depicting the hotel in Sasuelo, while the second is from *Running Away* (2005), and describes a hotel in Portoferraio.

In *The Bathroom*, for fifteen pages or so, I did my utmost to hide the fact that the hotel was in Venice. I never gave a thought to finding it a plausible site in the city, an *actual place* to build it in (the Zattere, for instance), nor even an *imaginary place* where it might be erected. The hotel had neither lobby nor façade nor sign, it was a purely mental hotel, a view from the mind; all that interested me was the room, the inside of the room where the narrator had locked himself. Beyond that room, I built a network of corridors, bends, landings, and floors ("it was a labyrinth, no signs indicating anything anywhere"). The other rooms only appeared in the book according to my novelistic needs, in successive layers, not so much to try and construct a harmonious and functional architectural ensemble, but according to the rhythm of the scenes I was writing, each room being created only for its *fictional function*.

The founding image of *Making Love* was a brief conversation between the narrator and Marie in front of the great picture window of a hotel in Shinjuku, Tokyo. The book was built on that image; it had forced itself on me as I was walking down the steep little path of the Tour d'Agnello in Corsica. I knew right away that image would give birth to a book, not a film, for it was a literary image, made of words, of adjectives and verbs, not cloth, flesh, and light. The way I built that hotel in Tokyo is entirely representative of the way I build my hotels, which is to say—the way I build my characters. For from a literary point of view, there is no difference between building a hotel and building a character. In both cases, details from reality merge with images that form in the imagination, fantasy, or reverie; sometimes a few sketches will be added, doodles, photos, more traditional documents, travel guides, a detailed map of Tokyo, brochures that help me locate hotels in space and copy out their exact address (2-7-2, Nishi-Shinjuku, Shinjuku-ku). I only ever make up a hotel from several existing hotels. I mix them up and melt them together to form one of my liking, feeding my imagination authentic details drawn from real life, which will graft themselves onto my hotel-in-progress. This is as true of my hotels as it is of my characters—I make as if I'm talking about hotels, but I'm actually talking about Edmondsson or Marie. In the same way that it takes several hundred pounds of aromatic shrubs to produce, by distillation, a vial of essence of rosemary, a great deal of real life must be extinguished to obtain the concentrate that is a single page of fiction. This network of multiple influences, various autobiographical sources, which merge, overlap, braid, and gather until you can't tell true from false, fiction from autobiography, feeds as much on dreams as memories, as much on desire as reality. Such a mixture of influences is particularly striking in the case of the hotel in Tokyo, where the room was inspired by a hotel room where I'd lived in Osaka, and the outside by a hotel I knew in Tokyo, which makes at least two hotels that served as models to build this imaginary hotel, not counting more hotels still, in Sendai or Shinagawa, from which I borrowed, here and there, some final detail (the scene with the TV set that turns itself on to warn of an incoming fax was inspired by something that really happened to me in a hotel in Shinagawa). And so, as in film, where it is common to blend several places together to make a single setting, the interior and exterior of the hotel were from different sources, but made a new ensemble, a hybrid building, fanciful and literary, an immaterial construct of adjectives and stone, words and steel, marble, crystal, and tears.

Literature and Cinema

I must have given a good dozen lectures called "Literature and Cinema" in my life, and up till now, I think I've always been slightly disappointing ("up till now"—I like the sound of that). Not that I have clear memories of some failed lecture where my repeated blunders made me the target of various perishable projectiles, sea cucumbers and catcalls rocketing across the lecture hall— no, nothing like that. Once, only once, I almost fainted onstage at NYU, just a dizzy spell, fleeting social vertigo (whatever was I doing there? was it really worth it to go on speaking?) and, feeling cold sweat gaining steadily at my temples, I stopped mid-sentence and left the room, apologizing, only to return again a few minutes later, pale all over, and resume my performance in a changed voice before the mental ovations of a crowd thereafter won over to my cause (for audiences, of course, always rise to the defense of a speaker in distress—it's enough to put you off being brilliant).

One day, I gave a lecture on the topic at Princeton University. Right off the bat, from the first step you take on the compound of campus, down one of those long, silent, studious wooded avenues where squirrels and pupils alike go in all tranquility about their respective innocent tasks (reading and climbing trees, eating nuts and fornicating), Princeton has that college microcosm feel, where everyone knows each other, envies each other, chitchats with each other, and where, just around the next bend, you might run into a reincarnation of Pnin or some Humbert Humbert nonchalantly walking a rattletrap bike bedecked with plaid paniers, so weighty and pervasive is the feeling of inhabiting the twittering pages of a Nabokov novel. After giving my lecture to a small audience in the studious gloom of a little private library (a lecture soberly entitled "Literature and Cinema," whose content I will spare you to avoid too obvious a *mise en abyme*), I was invited to dinner in Princeton at a very good seafood restaurant trimmed with dark wood paneling where, a few tables away, writer and critic Edmund White was dining that night. But enough society page. At our table, presiding over the soirée, was the Chair of Princeton's French Department, and beside him, slightly to the left—and here, we are drawing ever so slowly closer to my point—was a Polish academic, a professor of biology, or physics (or maybe biophysics), who embarked at meal's end upon an anecdote that I, in turn, would like to relate, not *faithfully*, mind you, but to the contrary, *treacherously*, as *treacherously* as possible, adapting and enhancing it, modifying and embellishing it—in short, appropriating it, exactly as a successful film adaptation of a good book should always do.

Here is the anecdote: that morning, the Polish academic (stop me before I start describing him—one sets out to be an essayist, only inevitably to backslide toward fiction) was having a beverage with a few of his fellow professors in a café near campus, and as they were discussing this and that about the different subjects they taught, comparing the respective traits and merits of biology and math, one of the professors advanced the following hypothesis: that in his mind, one might say the differences between biology and math were the same as those between literature and cinema.

Now that, it seems to me, is a remarkable insight. It is true that the object of a mathematician's quest, or a writer's, is a perfect abstraction, an imaginary object, a pure fiction (using works from the past, and perhaps taking inspiration from reality, the mathematician and the writer build an ideal world whose rules they themselves devise), while the biologist and the filmmaker must compromise with reality; the objects of their quests are concrete, visible and measurable, tangible and quantifiable. Moreover, the mathematician and the writer, using their minds for the most part, work alone, needing no particular technical means (at the risk of exaggerating slightly, one could say all they need is paper and pen, or these days, a basic computer), while the biologist and the filmmaker, directing highly specialized teams (scientific laboratories or film crews), require heavy, often complicated and costly equipment. The mathematician and the writer have a tenuous connection with the world; they work in a universe free from constraint, their visions abstract, their equations immaterial; they advance slowly, often in a fog, all alone, beset by hesitation and doubt. The filmmaker and the biologist, on the other hand, have structured, reassuring social interactions; they are concretely confronted by the reality of things, both in the human aspect of their work (contact with teams they're in charge of, the search for funding), and in the very heart of their daily activity, which is always centered on the living (ah, actresses!). So we have, in one case, people who are remarkably well-balanced, responsible, and measured (biologists and filmmakers), and on the other, alas, anxiety-ridden, irresponsible, onanistic dreamers who've lost all touch with reality (I see the time has come to say a word about Proust).

Reading Proust

It is rare, I believe, to read the three thousand-some pages of *In Search of Lost Time* in a single sitting (sweet Christ, how can anyone write a book that long?). In fact, when I think about it, I realize *In Search of Lost Time* is one of those rare books I've read less often than re-read, regularly dipping into it over the years, no longer really knowing, ultimately, if I've already read at least once before certain passages I'm now re-reading.

In its richness and its exceptional dimensions, *In Search of Lost Time* is a book that accompanies us throughout our lives. Indeed, upon reading it, or re-reading it, or re-reading ten years later some passage I'd already read ten years before, or in coming upon another I no longer remember, or which I might never even have read, but which reminds me, in setting or character, of one already read, so closely are the two intertwined and intimately entangled in the colossal gossamer web of the work, something odd often happens to me—there springs to mind, exactly as if from the narrator's cup when he recognizes the taste of the morsel of madeleine soaked in lime-blossom tea, the very essence of the volume I was reading at the time, the smell and feel of its pages, the supple, malleable leather binding on the Pléiade edition I was reading back then, the lightness of its onionskin paper, but also the armchair I was sitting in, the entire room of my grandfather's apartment where I was then living, the long curtains of yellow velour with their frills and flounces, and the golden light of the reading lamp, the handsome Persian rug, the furniture, the bed, the glass-fronted library lined with books and stacked manuscripts. All this and more—the specific odor of that room, the mixture of dust and mustiness that briefly flits by my nostrils. This is in no way an act of memory, a mental effort or a feat of concentration, but rather pure magic, the same pure magic that sometimes, when chancing upon a taste or smell we've known in life, lets us conjure up a moment from the past into the present, and in so doing rediscover for the space of a few seconds, intact and unchanged—not in any considered, intellectual fashion, but rather one purely fortuitous, sensitive, and sensual—the essence of what has vanished forever (in other words, and in short, lost time).

I was about twenty when I attempted my first ascent of *In Search of Lost Time*, with much care and caution (as if the book, with its dimensions and reputation, were somehow intimidating, as if I weren't necessarily worthy of reading it myself yet, and I had to open it with a great deal of cautiousness) and, utterly cavalier, skipped the whole first part, "Combray," on my mother's advice, diving right into "Swann in Love," which was lighter and more novelistic, brighter, funnier, and livelier, with that ecstatic description of the little Verdurin clan right up front. It is indeed a fact that, for those first-time tacklers of such literary heights who are not, as I have by dint of reading and experience become over the years, one of the seasoned Annapurnas scrambling up and down the sheerest literary slopes with insectile agility (and several legendary peaks to their name, literature's most fabled twenty-thousand-footers already under their belt: *Ulysses*, *Under the Volcano*, *The Man Without Qualities*, *The Alexandria Quartet*), "Swann in Love" is without a doubt the simplest way of ascending *In Search of Lost Time*— the easiest, most basic, and best-marked route toward that summit of twentieth century literature.

Some six hundred pages later, six hundred pages further along, in a bungalow in the administrative complex of Ain d'Heb, not far from Médéa in Algeria, where the temperature was nearing 104°F in the shade, the window of the studio where I lived thrown wide open to the broad sunny terrace, I was reading *In the Shadow of Young Girls in Flower* in the shadow of tomato plants we were growing in our little garden. The stones, rough and uneven on the ground, were burning under the balls of my feet when, pausing my reading for a moment, I would get up and walk around, stretching or massaging my back; then, returning to the book I'd left open behind me on the chair, I would resume my reading in the cool shadow of the bungalow in Ain d'Heb. Sometimes, taking my schoolboy chair out on the terrace (most of the furniture at my disposal in that studio had been furnished by the high school where I taught and if, afternoons, I read in a schoolboy chair, evenings I would read in an iron-frame dorm bed I'd been lent, propped up on a pillow), I would settle down beside the little garden where I'd planted some lettuce and a few radishes, and in this way I read *In Search of Lost Time* in the emollient tepidity of late afternoon, as the sun sank gradually toward the horizon. Soon, in fact, there was no more shade on my feet (by then I must have been headed down the Guermantes way).

Just how many pages lie between that schoolboy chair in Ain d'Heb and the armchair in the bedroom of my grandfather's apartment where, almost thirty years ago, I first opened *In Search of Lost Time* and read the first line of the book (which, curiously enough, was not "For a long time, I went to bed early," for I had started with "Swann in Love"); how many pages lie between it and the turquoise blue armchair I'm looking at right now in the main room of the house in Barcaggio, where a few months ago I was re-reading a passage from *In Search of Lost Time* in the Bouquins edition (a sturdy all-terrain edition you can take to the beach or hiking through the brush); and how much time lies between it and still other armchairs in other towns, other countries; how many pages, all in all, how many written and how many read, how many selves, different and alike, lie between that first armchair in the bedroom of my grandfather's apartment where I first read Proust and this turquoise blue armchair I'm looking at right now in the house in Barcaggio? How much time and how many selves? I don't know; all I remember are a few armchairs, the gray-blue velour armchair in my grandfather's bedroom, the somewhat stiff schoolboy chair in the bungalow in Médéa, and the turquoise blue armchair, dusty and unmoving, that I'm looking at right now in the main room of the house in Barcaggio.

The best books are the ones where you remember the armchairs you sat in while reading them.

I, Rodion Romanovich Raskolnikov

I read *Crime and Punishment* for the first time in 1979, in Portugal, on my sister's recommendation. I was twenty-one and hadn't read much before, no literature, just a few rare pearls like Kafka's *The Metamorphosis* or Camus' *The Stranger*. I don't remember particularly liking *Crime and Punishment*. No, what I felt was far beyond love or admiration. Quite simply, my eyes were opened. A month later, I started writing. It was that book, it was *Crime and Punishment* that opened my eyes to the force literature could have, its powers, its force, its fascinating possibilities. By identifying with the character of Raskolnikov, by knowing the particular thrill of identifying with Rodion Romanovich Raskolnikov—for I identified with that terribly ambiguous character right off the bat—I myself was committing a murder. By killing that old woman—that "louse," the word is Raskolnikov's—I accompanied the killer down his path, I entered his thoughts, I was afraid with him, I went out with him, and I walked up the street, heart pounding, to the old woman's house, an ax hanging inside my coat from a noose specially sewn for the purpose (I loved that detail—practical, dizzying). In fictitiously killing that old woman in a book, I became aware for the first time of the terrible powers literature possessed. That character—that student, that murderer—was me. I felt, without yet being able to articulate it, that one of literature's main strengths, a *force majeure*, lay in its ambiguity. Literature was—always had to be—sulfur, incandescence, acid. My reading had disturbed me so deeply because I had identified with a murderer. With that book, a new horizon opened before me. Raskolnikov's crime had as much influence on his life as a fictional character as on my own as the real person of twenty-one that I was at the time. The old woman's murder in St. Petersburg was *formative*, as much for Raskolnikov's life as for my own—for him, in becoming a killer, and for me, in becoming a writer.

But something else became apparent to me while I was reading *Crime and Punishment*, something subterranean, secret, subliminal, something I wasn't aware of at first and couldn't name, something it took me a long time to identify. I think I hit upon it while reading the book again, thirty years after the first time: the way Dostoyevsky uses "later", "after the fact," the limited, selective immixing of the future in the present, which is called prolepsis in narratology and a flash-forward in film (the opposite of flashback). This brief intrusion of the future into the present induces a feeling of premonition in the character, and for the author, involves an idea of fate.

Later on, when he recalled that time and all that happened to him during those days, minute by minute, point by point, he was superstitiously impressed by one circumstance, which though in itself not very exceptional, always seemed to him afterwards the predestined turning-point of his fate. He could never understand and explain to himself why, when he was tired and worn out, when it would have been more convenient for him to go home by the shortest and most direct way, he had returned by the Hay Market where he had no need to go. It was obviously and quite unnecessarily out of his way, though not much so. It is true that it happened to him dozens of times to return home without noticing what streets he passed through. But why, he was always asking himself, why had such an important, such a decisive and at the same time such an absolutely chance meeting happened in the Hay Market (where he had moreover no reason to go) at the very hour, the very minute of his life when he was just in the very mood and in the very circumstances in which that meeting was able to exert the gravest and most decisive influence on his whole destiny? As though it had been lying in wait for him on purpose!*

I am utterly fascinated by this paragraph—the murder hasn't been committed yet—by the way Dostoyevsky can anticipate, or already knows, that Raskolnikov will later remember this exact moment. I could almost say this is why I loved *Crime and Punishment*, this very use of prolepsis (did I not fear discouraging the best intentions). For me, there is some miracle, some prestidigitation, some magic in it, but nothing of witchcraft

*___

Crime and Punishment, trans. Constance Garnett, p. 60-61 (P.F. Collier & Son, 1917)

or the supernatural, which is quite the opposite, terribly pedestrian, banal, and prosaic. The fascinating figure of speech, prolepsis, which I must have sensed my first time through without being able to name, can be found throughout *Crime and Punishment*, one might say almost a secret code. Examples are endless. For instance: "Anyway, when he tried later on to piece his recollections together, he learnt a great deal about himself from what other people told him." Or: "Later, much later, he still remembered those days." "Later on," "when he remembered that moment," "much later," "long after . . ." And I cannot keep myself from likening this sweet litany of temporal adverbs with the laters in my own books. After all, isn't the first line of *The Truth about Marie* "Later on, thinking back on the last few hours of that sweltering night, I realized we had made love at the same time, Marie and I, but not with each other"?

One of the most fascinating scenes in *Crime and Punishment* is the confession. It is a model of reticence (from the Latin *reticencia*, for stubborn silence), perhaps even the height of reticence, as per the first definition given in the *Dictionnaire Le Robert*: "voluntary omission of something that should be said; the thing omitted." For Raskolnikov's confession is not one of words. His crime is one he cannot name. When he goes over to Sonia's intending to confess to the murder, he is unable to articulate it; he must settle for with having her guess. Everything takes place in silence, in innuendo, in exchanged glances

("Both looked at each other for a minute and waited"), and that is how the scene ends, although Raskolnikov has still not said anything explicit: "'Have you guessed?' he whispered at last." And Sonia answers: "'Good God!' broke in an awful wail from her bosom. She sank helplessly on the bed with her face in the pillows." There. The confession has been made, though the crime was never named at any point. Indeed, all throughout the book, the crime is unspeakable, not only for Raskolnikov, but also for those close to him (Sonia, Razumihin); they can only catch occasional glimpses of it in his eyes, like some monstrous shadow that darkens the air between them for a moment, as when a cloud passes overhead and briefly blots out the sun. But stranger yet is that "the thing"—the crime, that crime so hard for the characters to name—seems unspeakable even for the author himself. Dostoevsky persists in circling it, always avoiding it, evading it, dodging it, while constantly implying it, consciously putting it front and center in the book's every action, no matter how slight. The crime in *Crime and Punishment* is a sphere whose center is everywhere and circumference is nowhere. It is a silent crime that the reader, like Raskolnikov, will have to name, in order to free himself from the tacit punishment he brings about.

In his notebooks, Dostoyevsky quite rightly says that without his crime, Raskolnikov could not have discovered in himself "such problems, such desires, such feelings, such needs, such aspirations, such growth." But beyond silence, a very real anguish arises in the reader's mind. This anguish is literally unbearable in *Crime and Punishment*, where we end up burning to tell someone, to confess, in order to bring the torment of threats and empty waiting to an end. I have the feeling Dostoyevsky says things plainly once and only once in *Crime and Punishment*, and that is in the novel's most famous scene, the one where the book's trinity finds itself reunited. There, in a striking image, gathered by the bedside in Sonia's room, are the murderer, the whore, and the Bible: "The candle-end was flickering out in the battered candlestick, dimly lighting up in the poverty-stricken room the murderer and the harlot who had so strangely been reading together the eternal book." "The murderer," Dostoyevsky the writer calls Raskolnikov, and the word rings out in our mind. And it is all the more striking because it is one of the few times Dostoyevsky says things explicitly, so clearly names Raskolnikov a killer and Sonia a whore.

With *Crime and Punishment*, I discovered the power of literature, not its finesse. Only later did I take an interest in literature's actual stakes, issues of form, style, rhythm, structure: subtlety and refinement. Dostoevsky is probably not a great stylist. But it doesn't matter. I took *Crime and Punishment* right to the jaw. "A book must be an ax for the frozen sea within," said Kafka. An ax? In *Crime and Punishment*, I saw the bright blade of that ax — literature — gleaming for the first time.

The Day I Met
Jérôme Lindon

A telegram proved to be my first connection to Jérôme Lindon, I can still see the pale, blue-tinged sheet and the impersonal, machine-written words on the small strips of white paper stuck one beside the next, I read it over by the fireplace in that house in Erbalunga, and tried to contain my excitement, I no longer know exactly what was written in that telegram, it must have been a very simple message, doubtless Jérôme Lindon asking me to call him back, but I remember that, gazing at that piece of paper in my hands, I felt a strange calm, a presentiment that it held the confirmation *in potentia* of my life's direction.

I did not speak with Jérôme Lindon until the next day, from a small phone booth in the Erbalunga post office. I can perfectly recall the first words of that conversation, me scrunched up in the glass booth inside the post office, one hand on the receiver so as not to miss a word, and him asking me right up front if I'd already signed a contract with a publisher. No, the manuscript of *The Bathroom* had been turned down by every publishing house I'd sent it to, and it had lain waiting in the office of Alain Robbe-Grillet, who was then teaching in the U.S., Jérôme Lindon coming upon it only by accident one day as he was busying himself about the building (watering can in hand—who knows? When I later met him, he could very well have made that line of Beckett's his own — I'm quoting from memory now, it's in "The Expelled" or maybe *Molloy* — "I alone in that household understood something about tomatoes.").

From that day on, and for the entire month that followed — I had mailed the signed contract back, but we hadn't yet met — he would call me in Corsica once or twice a week, at my neighbors' who lived on the little farm below the house where I was living (it took five minutes to walk there, and five minutes back). I would turn up delighted and out of breath, and we would chat about this and that on the phone, my literary influences, my manuscript. At the time, it seemed natural to me that an editor be so interested in every last Lilliputian detail of a manuscript by an unknown writer. On Christmas Day, 1984, he even called me in Brussels at my parents' with a tiny reservation about which phrasing to prefer between "for him, a sinusitis was a very ordinary thing" and "for him, a sinusitis was but an ordinary thing." Certainly, he might have rung the night before, but showing great courtesy, had decided to wait till the next morning, no doubt deeming that the question could wait till lunch on December 25th.

We met at last on an afternoon in December, 1984. How very well I remember the first look Jérôme Lindon gave me that day, incredibly direct — right from the first time our eyes met, I was aware of an infallible gaze, a gaze that assessed, gauged, and judged. I'd been facing him for all of five seconds, he'd just risen from his chair to receive me in his office on the fourth floor of the rue Bernard-Palissy, and was in the middle of asking me, with the feeling of urgency, curiosity, and keenness that made him such a great editor, if I was taller than he was. But his bearing let nothing slip, he remained impassive and asked me to sit down, his face showed no disappointment when he noticed that I was very slightly taller than him: perhaps some minuscule repressed ruffle, a fleeting feeling of bitterness immediately banished from his mind (hmph, young authors these days lack respect for their elders, even the basic courtesy of being slightly shorter than their editors).

I don't remember much else about our first conversation, but I can still picture his office quite clearly: along the walls, shelves of books either white and blue with the Minuit star or in countless colored jackets, translations of his authors. Many new things began for me that day which would become ritual and immutable: meeting him at half past noon for lunch, his hurtle down the stairs to greet visitors and shake their hands, his slight breathlessness after such a dash, the slow walk to Le Sybarite, exchanging news and little pleasantries en route to the restaurant, his way of evading these and starting up the conversation again after a moment's silence. Something else I remember, something that struck me straightaway, was his capacity to defuse tensions with a mixture of authoritarian assurance in his eyes that commanded respect, and a gentility of gesture, in the glide of his hands and the velvetiness of his voice, which appeased people and preemptively warded off possible swipes of their claws, in the manner of a tamer toughened from working with the particularly vulnerable, dangerous, and unpredictable big cats that writers—I was starting to get the feeling—must be.

As I made my way from that first meeting on a late December afternoon in 1984, my strength left me little by little—too many things were happening at once, too many emotions—and I sat down on the sidewalk of the rue de Rennes, it was Christmas Eve, it was night, decorations hung from wires in shop windows, I was sitting by the edge of the road, brow damp with sweat, car headlights passing over my face, my gaze fogged over, and I felt myself slowly fainting, with my eyes I followed the taillights of cars driving off into the distance down the boulevard Saint-Germain, I looked at the sky, I looked at the city, I'd turned the collar of my coat up and I wasn't moving anymore, I was sitting there in the street in Paris around six p.m., I was twenty-seven, soon to be twenty-nine, I had just left a meeting with Jérôme Lindon, and *The Bathroom* was going to be published by Les Éditions de Minuit.

For Samuel Beckett

In the early '80s, I wrote Samuel Beckett a letter. I explained that I was trying to write, adding that he was probably often sought out by strangers, and so rather than asking him to read my work, suggested instead that we play a game of correspondence chess with, at stake, a play I'd written. If I won, he'd read it and give me his opinion. If he won, I'd read over my own play at my leisure. I closed my letter with these words: "Just in case, 1. e4." By return post, Samuel Beckett replied, "Black resigns. Send the play. Sincerely. Samuel Beckett." I sent him my play, and one or two weeks later, I got another handwritten note: he had kept his word, read my play, and advised me to trim certain passages.

Later—much later, by the scale on which I then perceived time (four years later, let's say)—I found myself in Jérôme Lindon's office on the rue Bernard-Palissy in Paris. My first novel, *The Bathroom*, had just come out to critical acclaim and our relations were most relaxed and cordial. At the end of our meeting, I rise and offer him my hand to take my leave. "You're in quite a hurry," he says. "Sit down, let's keep chatting a bit." I sit down, and we keep talking. The conversation flounders a little; I couldn't quite guess what he had in mind (apparently he was up to something). At exactly three p.m., the phone rings, and Jérôme Lindon hurls himself at his desk to get it (but he always had a precipitous way of picking up the phone, as if it were a matter of grabbing the contraption speedily, before it evaporated), and says, in a calm voice, "I'm coming down." He hangs up and says, "Come, I'll introduce you to Beckett." One behind the other, we go down the dark, steep spiral stairwell at Les Éditions de Minuit and there he is, Samuel Beckett, in the doorway to the first floor. I am extremely intimidated. I no longer know what Lindon is saying to him, I no longer know what I'm saying, I no longer know what Beckett is saying; in short, I don't know anything anymore. Some memoirist I am. In my memory—but maybe it's not even a memory, just a vague attempt to reconstruct the scene—we shake hands standing in the doorway, and three things strike me all at once: first off, Beckett's extremely weak and fragile legs, then the coat he's wearing that day, which I can still picture now— short, finely dotted with gray wool—and finally, perhaps the most eccentric thing for me (but fairly natural when you think about it, all things considered), when Beckett speaks French, he has an Irish accent.

In the years that follow, I will cross paths with Samuel Beckett again, once or twice, in the offices of the Éditions de Minuit, always in the same place, in the first floor doorway on the rue Bernard-Palissy (once, my sister is there too). Up till then, I had never sent my books to Beckett (out of modesty, or embarrassment, or shyness, I'm not sure), but with my third book, *Camera*, I feel a little more confident, and as it's been four years already since I've been speaking regularly about Beckett with Jérôme Lindon when we have lunch together, since I've asked after him without fail, and Lindon has had several occasions to let Beckett know how highly I admire his work, I tell Lindon that I'd like to sign a copy of my book for Beckett. Finally, and not at all lightly (I must have spent more time thinking about the dedication than writing the book, relatively speaking), I write: "For Samuel Beckett, with my immense esteem, my immense respect, and my immense admiration." Very good, says Lindon, I'll bring him the book. Beckett was already in a very weakened state in that month of January 1989, but Jérôme Lindon reported that he was very touched by my dedication. Later, I even found out through Jérôme Lindon, who visited him daily—and this scene requires much modesty to relate, though even more emotion to imagine—that, as Beckett was very weak and bedridden, Jérôme Lindon read the end of *Camera* aloud to him one day in his room.

Jérôme Lindon died in April 2001, and one day in 2002, as I was walking around the cemetery in Montparnasse looking for his grave, I chanced upon that of Beckett, who is buried nearby. The weather was beautiful. Gardeners were busy hosing down the gravestones. I came to a halt and, for a long time, stood in the path gazing at the smooth wet marble surface of of Beckett's tombstone, shining in the sun.

The Ravanastron

A ravanastron hung, on the wall, from a nail, like a plover.

A what? A ravanastron. The word unexpectedly appeared to me one day at the bottom of page 71 in *Watt*. It was like a dizzying bedazzlement, a pang of pleasure, a riddle and a challenge; the mysterious word was instantly graven in my memory (erroneously, in fact — for a long time, quite lightly, I said zavanastron instead of ravanastron). A zavanastron, then, if you're not a particular stickler.

A ravanastron hung, on the wall, from a nail, like a plover.

Enamored of the sentence's admirable balance, I still wondered, sometimes, what it could mean. Any dictionary would, if needed, tell me what a plover was, but a ravanastron? No. I fine-toothed Larousse, exhausted Robert, leafed through Le Littré ... nothing (it didn't help that I was always looking for a ravanastron under Z). Finally, I wound up opening my heart to Jérôme Lindon about it — how well I can still see the scene, at Le Sybarite, no doubt (we would lunch at that restaurant for all eternity, the only thing changing, the *plat du jour*). After a moment's reflection, brought up short by the question (fairly loony, it's true), and even more confused by what I meant since I kept saying zavanastron instead of ravanastron, Jérôme Lindon, with a vexed pout and a vague wavelike flutter of his hand, as if to shoo an invisible mosquito pestering him, said he guessed Beckett had found the word in one of the countless encyclopedias he was so fond of, but I'll ask him, I'll ask him, he said, I'll ask Sam. I never heard a word about it again.

Truth to tell, I didn't really give a damn what a ravanastron was. I didn't even know what a plover was. I mean at the time, of course. A wall, sure, I could see that. A nail—no problem. After all, I'd written several books myself. But I confess the first time I read that sentence, from those two familiar words, wall and nail, hung those two fascinating words, delightful-sounding and vaguely insolent, plover and ravanastron, "And the single string of the tromba marina"—never really understood what that meant either, mind you (to stick with musical instruments). Besides, now that I know what the sentence means, can attest that it has a meaning and even, if need be, ruin that meaning with an explanation, I realize that it is the form of the sentence, and not its meaning at all, that dazzled me so. Back then, by reading attentively, I could already picture what the sentence was supposed to describe, picture a wall, picture a nail in the wall, but knowing neither what a plover nor a ravanstron was, the image that began gently taking shape in the cottony mists of my mind remained purely abstract, a pure giddiness of sound and rhythm, a mental rattle of colors and consonants—literature itself, my lambkins.

On Bus 63

My knowledge of Beckett's body of work is very approximate, incomplete, lacunal, full of flaws and contradictions, mixed-up names, vagueness about how anecdotes go and haziness about their chronology. "Vagueness I abhor," Molloy would have said (or Malone, I don't know — me and references). But this imprecision counts for little beside the shock, vivid as ever, whose attenuated waves I still feel today, the shock I felt thirty years ago upon encountering the work of Samuel Beckett. It is the most important reading experience of my life. My only model, I told Jérôme Lindon when he published my first novel. I didn't, strictly speaking, identify with Beckett's characters — not with Molloy, or Malone — but I realized, reading Beckett, that here was one possible way of writing. Other writers I admired — Proust, Kafka, Dostoevsky — I could admire without wanting to write like them, but Beckett was the first time I found myself in the presence of a writer I unconsciously felt I had to challenge, confront, from whose grip I had to free myself. Without really being conscious of it, I started writing like Beckett (which is no way to go about trying to write, for no matter who you are, you're better off writing like yourself). I hit a wall; I went through a period of depression and despondency. It was a painful ordeal, but a salutary one. I had to rid myself of that pivotal influence, that terribly lucid gaze on the world — a black, Pascalian gaze, but also a bearer of energy and triumphant humor.

In a way, Beckett's work is unapproachable, or to put it another way, all the usual ways of discussing a book are here rendered null, inappropriate, moronic, ineffective. In general, when discussing a book, we bring up the story. Here story is absent, and plot, anecdote, reduced to a minimum. Story is not at stake; that isn't the issue, isn't the important part. It would be vain and foolhardy (or "frivolous and vexatious," to take up Beckett's tasty adjectives from *Murphy*) to try and summarize the stories of *Molloy*, *Malone Dies*, and *The Unnamable*. Of necessity, we fail at replacing words with other words when it comes to Beckett. "I love the word, words have been my only loves, not many" (*Têtes-mortes*). Historical context is just as absent from Beckett's work; there are no allusions to political situation or social context; we are in a pure time preserved from history, we are in an atemporal world. But where are we, then? In a consciousness, it seems to me, in Beckett's mind; we are fly-by travelers through Beckett's mind, and spend a few happy hours there, the time it takes us to read. The characters we meet—the Molloys, Morans, Malones, Mahoods, Worms—are barely characterized, save for their infinite infirmities, which verge on exhausting the physical woes that can afflict us. They take turns speaking, but aren't really differentiated, seem interchangeable; Molloy and Moran seem reflections of each other, one could pass for the other's projection, the product of his imagination, his dream or his conscience. I'd go even farther and say that to varying degrees they are all representatives of a single narrator. Here is my hypothesis: in Beckett's trilogy, just as in *In Search of Lost Time*, there is just one narrator; I use the very Proustian term "narrator" on purpose. And if Gérard Genette was able to sum up the entire *Search* with his radical "Marcel becomes a writer," we might, using the same model, sum up the entire trilogy with the simple "Molloy must go on," for right from the first line of the first book—"I am in my mother's room. It's I who live there now. I don't know how I got there. Perhaps in an ambulance, certainly a vehicle of some kind"—Molloy cannot go on, but Molloy must go on, and Molloy will go on. Go on with what? That isn't specified. He must go on, that's all. Go on. Living? Dying (Malone)? Looking for Molloy (Moran)? Writing? Speaking? ("And at the same time I am obliged to speak. I shall never be silent. Never.") To go on. As if for Beckett, the phrasal verb needed no further complement. Throughout these three books, shedding or changing names like molts that fall one after the next with successive sloughing, becoming Moran or Malone, in the end becoming no more than a voice—the voice of the narrator that ends up breaking through and freeing itself from all the straw men it's devised, the voice of the Unnameable that ends up naming them as well, all the Murphys and their ilk, "when I think of the time I've wasted with these bran-dips, beginning with Murphy . . . when I had me, on the premises, tottering under my own skin and bones, real ones, rotting with solitude and neglect"—throughout these books, Molloy goes on, he keeps at it, he must go on, he knows he can't go on, he knows he will go on. "You must go on, I can't go on, I'll go on." It could have been the first line of *Molloy*; it is the last line of *The Unnamable*.

As with any great author, as with any great book, it is in questions of rhythm, dynamics, energy, the standards of the form, that the book plays out. This trail was blazed by Flaubert a century ago, when he dreamed of a book about nothing ("a book with no external attachment, one that would hold together by the internal strength of its style, as the earth floats in the air unsupported"). But even this Flaubertian "nothing," as the ultimate exploitable material for a novel—even this, Beckett seems to mistrust. Beckett mistrusts the charms of "nothing" just as he mistrusts the tools that might express it. He takes aim only at the essential, stripping language down to the bone to approach an unattainable language. If he chooses to write in French, it is because French seems to him a language where one can write without style, while English would offer him too much occasion for virtuosity. But there is, I think, something more in Beckett's work, something that situates itself *beyond* even language. Beyond language, what remains in a book when one has made abstractions of the characters and story? The author remains, a solitude remains, a voice at once human and neglected. Beckett's work is fundamentally human; it expresses something of the wellspring of human truth at its purest. There are many writers we can admire, but very few we can, beyond literary admiration, simply love. And so the memory comes back to me of a poem by Villon which, from a distance of five hundred years, sometimes has the ring of Beckett; which reaches us on a breath of wind mingled with creaking from the ropes of hanged men:

> You see us five, six, hanging here
> As for the flesh we loved too well
> A while ago it was eaten and has rotted away [...]
> The rain has rinsed and washed us
> The sun dried us and turned us black
> Magpies and ravens have pecked out our eyes
> And plucked our beards and eyebrows

The first line of Villon's poem is "Brother humans, who live after us," and in that "brother human," I seem to recognize the feeling I get from reading Beckett: that of having found a brother human.

And yet for all that, Beckett's work isn't difficult; it is within the grasp of a child of twenty-three. I was twenty-three when I discovered Beckett's books, I was living in Paris in my grandfather's apartment. I read *Molloy* in a wing chair (or a Gainsborough chair, *noblesse oblige*) of aging pale blue velour, the upholstery on the arms slightly worn, in the bedroom of that apartment on the rue de Longchamp. I see myself in that armchair again, *Molloy* in my hands, the thick cover, the very dark letters, the big, beautiful capitals (J, C, M, Q), and here and there, commas big as jumbo shrimp, strewn among the sentences, dividing them up impeccably. Beside this rococo armchair is a lawn chair that could take its rightful place in the storage locker of my memory, the green cast-iron lawn chair on which I read *The Unnamable* on a sunny path in the Trocadero gardens, the sentences now merging with the setting in my mind, while in my memory, the unbroken babble of water in the garden's fountains that accompanied my reading fades away. But this mysterious alchemy between a book and a place was at its most radical with *Malone Dies*. I can't remember a precise scene from *Malone Dies*, but I have an absolute memory of reading the book, as if all my impressions of reading Beckett's work—scattered, confused, unformulated, my jumbled feelings of happiness, admiration, recognition—had crystallized at that exact moment in time and come together on an afternoon in 1981 on bus 63, which I'd just boarded to meet Madeleine on the rue des Fossés-Saint-Jacques. I'd been working all day in my grandfather's bedroom, and I was reading *Malone Dies* on the bus; I was still at the very beginning, I don't know what part I was reading—what did I read that was so striking that the sensation of that moment in time remains alive and intact thirty years later? I don't know. But that is where the scene must be set, if set it must be, visually, in an allegory representing my discovery of Beckett's work. It was a bedazzlement, a revelation, a call, a conversion; one thinks of Saint Paul falling from his horse on the road to Damascus. Here is the image: I was twenty-three and had just gotten off the bus at the intersection of the boulevard Saint-Germain and the rue Saint-Jacques; I'd closed *Malone Dies* a few moments ago, and I was struck down on the spot, flat on the sidewalk, my face ecstatic, full of light, my arms out in a cross like Caravaggio's St. Paul in the painting in Santa Maria del Popolo in Rome—and, instead of the horse, there is bus 63, peeling away into traffic towards the Seine, slowly vanishing from my memory.

JEAN-PHILIPPE TOUSSAINT is the author of several novels and the winner of numerous literary prizes, including the Prix Décembre for *The Truth About Marie*.

MICHAL AJVAZ, *The Golden Age.*
  The Other City.

PIERRE ALBERT-BIROT, *Grabinoulor.*

YUZ ALESHKOVSKY, *Kangaroo.*

FELIPE ALFAU, *Chromos.*
  Locos.

JOE AMATO, *Samuel Taylor's Last Night.*

IVAN ÂNGELO, *The Celebration.*

The Tower of Glass.

ANTÓNIO LOBO ANTUNES, *Knowledge of Hell.*
  The Splendor of Portugal.

ALAIN ARIAS-MISSON, *Theatre of Incest.*

JOHN ASHBERY & JAMES SCHUYLER,
  A Nest of Ninnies.

ROBERT ASHLEY, *Perfect Lives.*

GABRIELA AVIGUR-ROTEM, *Heatwave and Crazy Birds.*

DJUNA BARNES, *Ladies Almanack.*
  Ryder.

JOHN BARTH, *Letters.*
  Sabbatical.

DONALD BARTHELME, *The King.*
  Paradise.

SVETISLAV BASARA, *Chinese Letter.*

MIQUEL BAUÇÀ, *The Siege in the Room.*

RENÉ BELLETTO, *Dying.*

MAREK BIEŃCZYK, *Transparency.*

ANDREI BITOV, *Pushkin House.*

ANDREJ BLATNIK, *You Do Understand.*
  Law of Desire.

LOUIS PAUL BOON, *Chapel Road.*
  My Little War.
  Summer in Termuren.

ROGER BOYLAN, *Killoyle.*

IGNÁCIO DE LOYOLA BRANDÃO,
  Anonymous Celebrity.
  Zero.

BONNIE BREMSER, *Troia: Mexican Memoirs.*

CHRISTINE BROOKE-ROSE,
  Amalgamemnon.

BRIGID BROPHY, *In Transit.*

GERALD L. BRUNS,
  Modern Poetry and the Idea of Language.

GABRIELLE BURTON, *Heartbreak Hotel.*

MICHEL BUTOR, *Degrees.*
  Mobile.

G. CABRERA INFANTE, *Infante's Inferno.*
  Three Trapped Tigers.

JULIETA CAMPOS, *The Fear of Losing Eurydice.*

ANNE CARSON, *Eros the Bittersweet.*

ORLY CASTEL-BLOOM, *Dolly City.*

LOUIS-FERDINAND CÉLINE, *North.*
  Conversations with Professor Y.
  London Bridge.

MARIE CHAIX, *The Laurels of Lake Constance.*

HUGO CHARTERIS, *The Tide Is Right.*

ERIC CHEVILLARD, *Demolishing Nisard.*
  The Author and Me

MARC CHOLODENKO, *Mordechai Schamz.*

JOSHUA COHEN, *Witz.*

EMILY HOLMES COLEMAN, *The Shutter of Snow.*

ERIC CHEVILLARD, *The Author and Me.*

ROBERT COOVER, *A Night at the Movies.*

STANLEY CRAWFORD, *Log of the S.S. The Mrs Unguentine.*
  Some Instructions to My Wife.

RENÉ CREVEL, *Putting My Foot in It.*

RALPH CUSACK, *Cadenza.*

NICHOLAS DELBANCO, *Sherbrookes.*
  The Count of Concord.

NIGEL DENNIS, *Cards of Identity.*

PETER DIMOCK, *A Short Rhetoric for Leaving the Family.*

ARIEL DORFMAN, *Konfidenz.*

COLEMAN DOWELL, *Island People. Too Much Flesh and Jabez.*

ARKADII DRAGOMOSHCHENKO, *Dust.*

RIKKI DUCORNET, *Phosphor in Dreamland. The Complete Butcher's Tales. The Jade Cabinet. The Fountains of Neptune.*

WILLIAM EASTLAKE, *The Bamboo Bed. Castle Keep. Lyric of the Circle Heart.*

JEAN ECHENOZ, *Chopin's Move.*

STANLEY ELKIN, *A Bad Man. Criers and Kibitzers, Kibitzers and Criers. The Dick Gibson Show. The Franchiser. The Living End. Mrs. Ted Bliss.*

FRANÇOIS EMMANUEL, *Invitation to a Voyage.*

PAUL EMOND, *The Dance of a Sham.*

SALVADOR ESPRIU, *Ariadne in the Grotesque Labyrinth.*

LESLIE A. FIEDLER, *Love and Death in the American Novel.*

JUAN FILLOY, *Op Oloop.*

ANDY FITCH, *Pop Poetics.*

GUSTAVE FLAUBERT, *Bouvard and Pécuchet.*

KASS FLEISHER, *Talking out of School.*

JON FOSSE, *Aliss at the Fire. Melancholy.*

FORD MADOX FORD, *The March of Literature.*

MAX FRISCH, *I'm Not Stiller. Man in the Holocene.*

CARLOS FUENTES, *Christopher Unborn. Distant Relations. Terra Nostra. Where the Air Is Clear.*

TAKEHIKO FUKUNAGA, *Flowers of Grass.*

WILLIAM GADDIS, JR., *The Recognitions.*

JANICE GALLOWAY, *Foreign Parts. The Trick Is to Keep Breathing.*

WILLIAM H. GASS, *Life Sentences. The Tunnel. The World Within the Word. Willie Masters' Lonesome Wife.*

GÉRARD GAVARRY, *Hoppla! 1 2 3.*

ETIENNE GILSON, *The Arts of the Beautiful. Forms and Substances in the Arts.*

C. S. GISCOMBE, *Giscome Road. Here.*

DOUGLAS GLOVER, *Bad News of the Heart.*

WITOLD GOMBROWICZ, *A Kind of Testament.*

PAULO EMÍLIO SALES GOMES, *P's Three Women.*

GEORGI GOSPODINOV, *Natural Novel.*

JUAN GOYTISOLO, *Count Julian. Juan the Landless. Makbara. Marks of Identity.*

HENRY GREEN, *Blindness. Concluding. Doting. Nothing.*

JACK GREEN, *Fire the Bastards!*

JIŘÍ GRUŠA, *The Questionnaire.*

MELA HARTWIG, *Am I a Redundant Human Being?*

JOHN HAWKES, *The Passion Artist. Whistlejacket.*

ELIZABETH HEIGHWAY, ED.,
Contemporary Georgian Fiction.

AIDAN HIGGINS, *Balcony of Europe.*
Blind Man's Bluff.
Bornholm Night-Ferry.
Langrishe, Go Down.
Scenes from a Receding Past.

KEIZO HINO, *Isle of Dreams.*

KAZUSHI HOSAKA, *Plainsong.*

ALDOUS HUXLEY, *Antic Hay.*
Point Counter Point.
Those Barren Leaves.
Time Must Have a Stop.

NAOYUKI II, *The Shadow of a Blue Cat.*

DRAGO JANČAR, *The Tree with No Name.*

MIKHEIL JAVAKHISHVILI, *Kvachi.*

GERT JONKE, *The Distant Sound.*
Homage to Czerny.
The System of Vienna.

JACQUES JOUET, *Mountain R.*
Savage.
Upstaged.

MIEKO KANAI, *The Word Book.*

YORAM KANIUK, *Life on Sandpaper.*

ZURAB KARUMIDZE, *Dagny.*

JOHN KELLY, *From Out of the City.*

HUGH KENNER, *Flaubert, Joyce and Beckett: The Stoic Comedians.*
Joyce's Voices.

DANILO KIŠ, *The Attic.*
The Lute and the Scars.
Psalm 44.
A Tomb for Boris Davidovich.

ANITA KONKKA, *A Fool's Paradise.*

GEORGE KONRÁD, *The City Builder.*

TADEUSZ KONWICKI, *A Minor Apocalypse.*
The Polish Complex.

ANNA KORDZAIA-SAMADASHVILI,
Me, Margarita.

MENIS KOUMANDAREAS, *Koula.*

ELAINE KRAF, *The Princess of 72nd Street.*

JIM KRUSOE, *Iceland.*

AYSE KULIN, *Farewell: A Mansion in Occupied Istanbul.*

EMILIO LASCANO TEGUI, *On Elegance While Sleeping.*

ERIC LAURRENT, *Do Not Touch.*

VIOLETTE LEDUC, *La Bâtarde.*

EDOUARD LEVÉ, *Autoportrait.*
Newspaper.
Suicide.
Works.

MARIO LEVI, *Istanbul Was a Fairy Tale.*

DEBORAH LEVY, *Billy and Girl.*

JOSÉ LEZAMA LIMA, *Paradiso.*

ROSA LIKSOM, *Dark Paradise.*

OSMAN LINS, *Avalovara.*
The Queen of the Prisons of Greece.

FLORIAN LIPUŠ, *The Errors of Young Tjaž.*

GORDON LISH, *Peru.*

ALF MACLOCHLAINN, *Out of Focus.*
Past Habitual.
The Corpus in the Library.

RON LOEWINSOHN, *Magnetic Field(s).*

YURI LOTMAN, *Non-Memoirs.*

D. KEITH MANO, *Take Five.*

MINA LOY, *Stories and Essays of Mina Loy.*

MICHELINE AHARONIAN MARCOM,
A Brief History of Yes.
The Mirror in the Well.

BEN MARCUS, *The Age of Wire and String.*

WALLACE MARKFIELD, *Teitlebaum's Window.*

DAVID MARKSON, *Reader's Block.*
Wittgenstein's Mistress.

CAROLE MASO, *AVA.*

HISAKI MATSUURA, *Triangle.*

LADISLAV MATEJKA & KRYSTYNA POMORSKA, EDS., *Readings in Russian Poetics: Formalist & Structuralist Views.*

HARRY MATHEWS, *Cigarettes.*
The Conversions.
The Human Country.
The Journalist.
My Life in CIA.
Singular Pleasures.
The Sinking of the Odradek.
Stadium.
Tlooth.

HISAKI MATSUURA, *Triangle.*

DONAL MCLAUGHLIN, *beheading the virgin mary, and other stories.*

JOSEPH MCELROY, *Night Soul and Other Stories.*

ABDELWAHAB MEDDEB, *Talismano.*

GERHARD MEIER, *Isle of the Dead.*

HERMAN MELVILLE, *The Confidence-Man.*

AMANDA MICHALOPOULOU, *I'd Like.*

STEVEN MILLHAUSER, *The Barnum Museum.*
In the Penny Arcade.

RALPH J. MILLS, JR., *Essays on Poetry.*

MOMUS, *The Book of Jokes.*

CHRISTINE MONTALBETTI, *The Origin of Man.*
Western.

NICHOLAS MOSLEY, *Accident.*
Assassins.
Catastrophe Practice.
A Garden of Trees.
Hopeful Monsters.
Imago Bird.
Inventing God.
Look at the Dark.
Metamorphosis.
Natalie Natalia.
Serpent.

WARREN MOTTE, *Fables of the Novel: French Fiction since 1990.*
Fiction Now: The French Novel in the 21st Century.
Mirror Gazing.
Oulipo: A Primer of Potential Literature.

GERALD MURNANE, *Barley Patch.*
Inland.

YVES NAVARRE, *Our Share of Time.*
Sweet Tooth.

DOROTHY NELSON, *In Night's City.*
Tar and Feathers.

ESHKOL NEVO, *Homesick.*

WILFRIDO D. NOLLEDO, *But for the Lovers.*

BORIS A. NOVAK, *The Master of Insomnia.*

FLANN O'BRIEN, *At Swim-Two-Birds.*
The Best of Myles.
The Dalkey Archive.
The Hard Life.
The Poor Mouth.
The Third Policeman.

CLAUDE OLLIER, *The Mise-en-Scène.*
Wert and the Life Without End.

PATRIK OUŘEDNÍK, *Europeana.*
The Opportune Moment, 1855.

BORIS PAHOR, *Necropolis.*

FERNANDO DEL PASO, *News from the Empire.*
Palinuro of Mexico.

ROBERT PINGET, *The Inquisitory.*
Mahu or The Material.
Trio.

MANUEL PUIG, *Betrayed by Rita Hayworth.*
The Buenos Aires Affair.
Heartbreak Tango.

RAYMOND QUENEAU, *The Last Days.*
Odile.
Pierrot Mon Ami.
Saint Glinglin.

JOSEF ŠKVORECKÝ, *The Engineer of Human Souls.*

GILBERT SORRENTINO, *Aberration of Starlight.*
Blue Pastoral.
Crystal Vision.
Imaginative Qualities of Actual Things.
Mulligan Stew. Red the Fiend.
Steelwork.
Under the Shadow.

MARKO SOSIČ, *Ballerina, Ballerina*

ANDRZEJ STASIUK, *Dukla.*
Fado.

GERTRUDE STEIN, *The Making of Americans.*
A Novel of Thank You.

LARS SVENDSEN, *A Philosophy of Evil.*

PIOTR SZEWC, *Annihilation.*

GONÇALO M. TAVARES, *A Man: Klaus Klump.*
Jerusalem.
Learning to Pray in the Age of Technique.

LUCIAN DAN TEODOROVICI, *Our Circus Presents . . .*

NIKANOR TERATOLOGEN, *Assisted Living.*

STEFAN THEMERSON, *Hobson's Island.*
The Mystery of the Sardine.
Tom Harris.

TAEKO TOMIOKA, *Building Waves.*

JOHN TOOMEY, *Sleepwalker.*

DUMITRU TSEPENEAG, *Hotel Europa.*
The Necessary Marriage.
Pigeon Post.
Vain Art of the Fugue.

ESTHER TUSQUETS, *Stranded.*

DUBRAVKA UGRESIC, *Lend Me Your Character.*
Thank You for Not Reading.

TOR ULVEN, *Replacement.*

MATI UNT, *Brecht at Night.*
Diary of a Blood Donor.
Things in the Night.

ÁLVARO URIBE & OLIVIA SEARS, EDS., *Best of Contemporary Mexican Fiction.*

ELOY URROZ, *Friction.*
The Obstacles.

LUISA VALENZUELA, *Dark Desires and the Others.*
He Who Searches.

PAUL VERHAEGHEN, *Omega Minor.*

BORIS VIAN, *Heartsnatcher.*

LLORENÇ VILLALONGA, *The Dolls' Room.*

TOOMAS VINT, *An Unending Landscape.*

ORNELA VORPSI, *The Country Where No One Ever Dies.*

AUSTRYN WAINHOUSE, *Hedyphagetica.*

CURTIS WHITE, *America's Magic Mountain.*
The Idea of Home.
Memories of My Father Watching TV.
Requiem.

DIANE WILLIAMS,
Excitability: Selected Stories.
Romancer Erector.

DOUGLAS WOOLF, *Wall to Wall.*
Ya! & John-Juan.

JAY WRIGHT, *Polynomials and Pollen.*
The Presentable Art of Reading Absence.

PHILIP WYLIE, *Generation of Vipers.*

MARGUERITE YOUNG, *Angel in the Forest.*
Miss MacIntosh, My Darling.

REYOUNG, *Unbabbling.*

VLADO ŽABOT, *The Succubus.*

ZORAN ŽIVKOVIĆ , *Hidden Camera.*

LOUIS ZUKOFSKY, *Collected Fiction.*

VITOMIL ZUPAN, *Minuet for Guitar.*

SCOTT ZWIREN, *God Head.*

AND MORE . . .